Mary P. Thompson

A Memoir of Judge Ebenezer Thompson of Durham, New Hampshire

with some account of his parentage and offspring

Mary P. Thompson

A Memoir of Judge Ebenezer Thompson of Durham, New Hampshire
with some account of his parentage and offspring

ISBN/EAN: 9783337368500

Printed in Europe, USA, Canada, Australia, Japan

Cover: Foto ©Andreas Hilbeck / pixelio.de

More available books at **www.hansebooks.com**

A MEMOIR

OF

JUDGE EBENEZER THOMPSON

OF

DURHAM, NEW HAMPSHIRE,

WITH SOME ACCOUNT OF HIS PARENTAGE AND
OFFSPRING.

BY HIS GREAT-GRANDDAUGHTER,

MARY P. THOMPSON.

"Tell me what ancestors were thine."
[*Farinata to Dante.*]
INFERNO,
Canto X.

Concord, N. H.

PRINTED BY THE REPUBLICAN PRESS ASSOCIATION.

1886.

JUDGE EBENEZER THOMPSON AND HIS PARENTAGE.

Among the prominent men in New Hampshire at the Revolutionary period was the Hon. Ebenezer Thompson, Councillor of the State under the temporary constitution, and again under the state constitution, member of the Committee of Safety, Judge for many years of the Court of Common Pleas, Justice of the Superior Court of Judicature, etc., etc. He is incontestably the most eminent man ever born in the town of Durham; for Gen. Sullivan, though a citizen, was not a native of the place.

Durham, however insignificant at the present moment, is one of the oldest towns in the state, and is noted in history for the repeated and cruel attacks of the Indians in the wars of the seventeenth and eighteenth centuries. It was then known as the Oyster River settlement, so called from a branch of the Piscataqua that flows directly through the hilly and somewhat picturesque village, which stands at the head of tide-water about two miles from the mouth of the river. Half a mile distant, towards Madbury, on a height slowly ascending all the way, is the Thompson homestead, that has always been in possession of the family from the first grant. The present mansion was built by Judge Thompson himself, on the site of an older one in which he was born. This house has been scrupulously kept unchanged in its principal features, and is now owned and occupied by his great-great-grandson. There are the same large rooms of hospitable aspect, characteristic of the builder, with low ceilings, heavy mouldings and cornices, huge shafts of timber framework in the corners, a good deal of wainscoting, small panes of glass in the windows, and in the "hall-chamber," specially reserved for guests, the same paper on the walls as a century ago.

The first house on this spot was built as early as 1721, by Judge Thompson's father, Robert by name, who is first mentioned as being at Oyster River in the year 1707. On the 17th of September in that year, Robert Thompson was with Capt. Samuel Chesley, a brave officer just returned from Port Royal, and eleven others, engaged in clearing the forest, when, as Belknap relates, they were suddenly attacked by a band of " French Mohawks painted red," who, with a terrific yell, fell suddenly upon them and killed eight or nine of their number,—among them Captain Chesley and his brother James. The Rev. John Pike, in his Journal, states that the Indian who killed James Chesley was slain on the spot by Robert Thompson.[1] The latter and three or four others were so fortunate as to escape uninjured.

The place where this attack occurred is about half a mile from the Thompson homestead, and now belongs to Ebenezer Thompson Emerson, a descendant of Robert Thompson in the female line. According to the barbarous custom at that time of giving a bounty for every Indian scalp, a vote was passed in the Provincial Assembly at Portsmouth, October 22, 1707, to give five pounds to Robert Thompson " for his encouragement in bringing in an Indian scalp."[2] It does not appear, however, that he availed himself of this "encouragement" in order to advance his fortunes, for it is the only scalp on record that he presented, though his name is to be found on the muster-roll of Col. James Davis[3] in 1712, showing that he took his turn in the scouting parties so necessary for the protection of the early settlements,—a service justly styled in the council-books an " honorable " one. He must have been an efficient member of these expeditions, for, according

---

[1] "Journal of the Rev. John Pike," edited by the Rev. A. H. Quint, D. D., page 34. Also the N. H. Provincial Papers, II : 565-6, *note*.

Belknap, in his account of this attack, does not mention Robert Thompson.

[2] N. H. Prov. Papers, Vol. III : 348, 366, 423.

[3] Robert Thompson afterwards married Col. Davis's niece.

to the tradition handed down in the family, he was a brave, active man, of stalwart proportions, with great powers of endurance and uncommon muscular strength. He so excelled in all athletic exercises that stories concerning them were related nearly a century after, by old men of the town, in order to amuse my brother in his childhood.

Notwithstanding Robert Thompson's constitutional bravery, his life seems to have been chiefly spent in peacefully clearing and cultivating his lands, and in establishing his children. It does not appear that he took any special part in the affairs of the town. His name, however, is found affixed to a document indicative of his interest in the moral and intellectual welfare of the place. This was a petition of the leading settlers to Lieut. Gov. Vaughan, in 1715, for a license to employ a school-master, and also to have a separate parish at Oyster River, with power to assess the people for the support of a minister; otherwise, as the document goes on to state, "we must be without one, and return to Dover again, which was thought a hardship more than forty years ago." And well it might have been thought a hardship, for the parish meeting-house was then at Dover Point, six or eight miles distant, and the way thither through marshes and the wild forest, where there was constant danger of attack by the Indians.

As Robert Thompson must have arrived at manhood, or nearly so, at the time of the Indian attack in 1707, he could not have been born later than 1688 or 1690. Strange to say, no record has been found of his birth, marriage, or the precise time of his death. It is certain, however, that he was married as early as 1722 to Abigail (b. Sept. 27, 1704), daughter of Capt. Samuel Emerson and of Judith Davis, his wife.[1]

Robert Thompson's wife, Abigail, belonged to a family that might be called historic. On both sides it suffered to an uncommon degree from the Indians, and a great number of its members took part in the various wars of last century. Her father was one of the first deacons chosen after the organization of a church at Oyster River, but is called " Captain " by the Rev. Hugh Adams in his records of the parish, conveying the idea that he wielded the carnal as well as the spiritual weapon, which no doubt he did, after the manner and necessity of those times. He was a native of Haverhill, Mass., and a brother of the

[1] There is a tradition of a previous marriage of Robert Thompson to Mary Huckins, but of this I find no record, and if it took place she must have died soon after, leaving no children. The Huckins family, however, owned land in the neighborhood, on which stood the garrison of their name, destroyed by the Indians in 1689, as related by Belknap; in which attack eighteen persons were killed, besides several children, who were put to death in a most barbarous manner. The place where this massacre occurred is now owned by Mr. J. W. Coe, a descendant of Judge Thompson in the female line.

heroic Hannah Dustan, who, taken captive by the Indians in their attack on Haverhill, March 15, 169⅞, and forced to march forty miles through the wilderness and see her infant's brains dashed out against a tree, slew ten of their number with their own tomahawks as they lay asleep,[1] and with the scalps made her way home in a canoe on the Merrimack.

In this same attack on Haverhill, Thomas, a brother of Capt. Samuel Emerson, was slain, together with his wife and two children, and his house burned to the ground.

In another attack on the same town, in 1701, his brother, Jonathan Emerson, bravely withstood the enemy and saved his garrison. He was one of the original grantees of Chester, N. H., where, in 1727 or 1728, he established his son Samuel, the first magistrate of that town, who, as Chase, in his History of Chester, says, "filled a place no other man has filled, or could fill." The inhabitants had so much confidence in his integrity and judgment that nearly all minor controversies were referred to him, and his decisions accepted without appeal to the law.[2]

---

[1] That is, with the aid of her nurse and a little boy, as is well known.

[2] Of the fifteen children of this Samuel Emerson, of Chester, the most prominent was Col. Nathaniel Emerson, of Candia, who filled many offices, both civil and military. During the Revolution he was very efficient in obtaining supplies and recruits for the Continental army, and was in constant correspond-

On the maternal side of Mrs. Robert Thompson's ancestry, her mother, Judith Emerson, was the daughter of John Davis (son of James Davis, who, in 1646, was the largest tax-payer in Haverhill, Mass., and a representative of that town to the General Assembly of Massachusetts Bay in 1660), who came to Dover as early as 1653, purchased land at Oyster River in 1656, was admitted freeman in Boston May 23, 1666, and was a selectman in Dover from 1663 to 1667, and in 1671. He had eleven children, of whom Judith was the youngest. Accord-

ence with Col. Folsom and the Committee of Safety. He took part in the battle of Bennington, and was made lieutenant-colonel in 1778.

Another son was Capt. Amos Emerson, of Chester, who received his commission at Ticonderoga, in 1776.

Capt. Nehemiah Emerson, of Haverhill, another grandson of the above Jonathan, served all through the Revolutionary war. He was at Bunker Hill, at Burgoyne's surrender, and was one of the guards at Major Andre's execution. From a private he rose to be a captain, and so won the esteem of his commanders that Washington himself spoke of him several years after as "a brave officer and a good disciplinarian."

To say nothing of the services of the many scattered branches of this family in the wars of last century, no less than ten of the Emersons of Haverhill alone served as officers or privates in the Seven Years War. Six were in Capt. Saltonstall's company in 1757,—Timothy Emerson as second lieutenant, Jonathan as sergeant, and the others as privates. James Emerson took part in the Canada expedition, and in marching from Crown Point to Ticonderoga, Dec. 20, 1760, fell through the ice, lost his pack, and narrowly escaped drowning. He was so frost-bitten that he was left behind, and was forty days in getting back to Haverhill.

ing to a constant family tradition, though I do not find her mentioned among the early captives, she was carried away by the Indians after her marriage, and held in captivity five years. A sister of hers was killed in the attack on Haverhill in 169⅚, together with her son. And when the Oyster River settlement was nearly destroyed in 1694, another sister was killed with her only son, and likewise her brother, Ensign John Davis,[1] together with his wife and several of his children. Two of his daughters, however, were carried into captivity. One of them, a mere child at the time, was adopted by the chief of the Abenaki tribe, but redeemed soon after by the Rev. Father Rasles, the noted Jesuit missionary among the Indians of Maine, afterwards so basely murdered by our troops in 1724. He baptized the young captive under the name of Mary Anne, and sent her to the Ursuline convent in Quebec to be educated. At the exchange of prisoners she refused to return home, saying, "This is the house of the Lord: here will I live, and here will I die." She took the veil Sept. 14, 1699, together with M'lle de Varennes, daughter of the governor of Trois Rivières. She died in 1749, after fifty years spent in the holy

---

[1] Ensign Davis's father, in his will, dated May 25, 1686, gives his son John "the six score acres of land which I had by a grant, situate and lying and being at Turtle pond in Oister river, and my best feather bed, the ticking and feathers, after the death of my wife."

exercises of the cloister, her age uncertain, but supposed to be about seventy.[1]

Colonel James Davis, another brother of Judith Emerson's, stoutly defended his garrison against the Indians in 1694, and succeeded in saving his family. For many years he was the companion of Col. Hilton in organizing and conducting scouting parties, and various expeditions for the defence of the colony, as related by Belknap, and was not only a brave officer, but an able magistrate, and had attained to the dignity of judge when he died in 1749.

Moses Davis, another brother, after escaping the massacre at Oyster River in 1694, was killed by the Indians thirty years later, June 10, 1724, together

[1] By some unaccountable mistake, it is stated in the "Histoire des Ursulines de Québec," Vol. I: 457-8, and also in the Abbé Tanguay's "Dictionnaire Généalogique," that Mary Anne Davis was from Salem. Her name was entered in the convent records as "M'lle Des Visses, from New England—Boston or the environs." Salem is not mentioned. There is not the slightest doubt, from the date and the circumstances of her captivity, as related in the above "Histoire," that she was from Oyster River. This has been acknowledged to the present writer by the accomplished author of that work. The knowledge of New England geography was very confused in those days, and to people at a distance every place along our coast, or in the vicinity of it, was considered near Boston.

Another Miss Davis, a captive from New England, and likewise baptized Mary Anne, became a nun at the Hôtel-Dieu in Quebec. She died in 1761, aged about 73, but whether she was a sister of the above mentioned Mary Anne or not is uncertain, though they were taken captive under similar circumstances, and about, if not actually, the same time.

with his son. His death was instantly avenged by a negro slave of his, who shot one of the leaders,—a son of the Baron de St. Castine, who had married the daughter of an Indian chief. This young chief had been a pupil of Father Rasles',—and Belknap, with the usual tendency of the time to asperse the character of such missionaries, implies that he bore a nearer relation; but for this there is no foundation whatever, as is now generally acknowledged. Love Davis, the daughter of Moses, in view of the fidelity of this slave to his master, gave orders that when he died he should be buried at her feet. This was done, and their graves are still pointed out at a short distance from Durham village.

It was in the midst of all these tragedies that Robert Thompson's wife was born and brought up; and her children, from their earliest years, heard them recounted by their grandmother, Judith Emerson, who ended her days with her daughter.

Robert Thompson, some time in the year 1752, dropped dead as he was walking in a path near his house. His wife survived him, and died in 1757. According to the inventory of his estate, he had considerable property, consisting chiefly of lands, not only in Durham, but in Rochester, Canterbury, and Lee (then a part of Durham), with certain rights in saw-mills and grist-mills in the last two places. He was likewise the owner of several negro slaves, never at any time very numerous in New Hampshire, three of whom are mentioned by name in the inventory of his estate, viz., John Battles (valued £350), Page (£120), and Nan (£350). A woman named Dinah is mentioned in his wife's inventory.

But perhaps the circumstances of the family, and its style of living, may be best shown by some account of the personal effects his wife left at her death. The details of her wardrobe, in particular, are somewhat curious, and show a surprising richness of dress for a remote country matron of those homespun times of supposed Puritanical simplicity, when the influence of the sumptuary laws against "intolerable excess and bravery of dress," so recently in force at Haverhill, where her parents had been brought up, was not wholly extinct.[1] But Durham, at that time, was in constant communication by river (then the great thoroughfare) with Portsmouth, where the residence of the governor and his council constituted a kind of vice-regal court that gave tone and fashion to the neighboring towns.

---

[1] The sumptuary laws in force at Haverhill in the XVII century forbade any one whose estate did not exceed £200 to wear any gold or silver lace or buttons, silk hoods, ribbons, or scarfs, etc., under the penalty of a fine. In 1653 the wife of John Hutchins, of Haverhill, was brought before a magistrate for wearing a silk hood, but "upon testimony of her being brought up above the ordinary way," was discharged. And as late as 1675, two daughters of Hannah Bosworth were fined ten shillings each for wearing silk dresses.

The following items from the inventory of Mrs. Thompson's estate have been carefully copied from the public records at Exeter, though differently arranged for the purpose of classification:

One gold necklace.
One pair of earrings.
Four gold rings.
One pair of gold sleeve-buttons.
One silver scissors-chain.
One silver snuff-box.
Two silver hair paggs.
One silver buckle and girdle.[1]
One golden girdle.
One fan (£4).
One scarlet riding-hood.
One brown riding-hood.
One scarlet cloak.
One brown cloak.
Two velvet hoods.
One flowered hood.
One silk bonnet.
Twenty-two yards of damask.
One brown damask gown.
One black damask gown.
One East India satin gown.
One yellow sarcenet gown.
One Persian (silk) gown.[2]
One tarltane gown.

---

[1] Silver was so scarce in New England in 1739 that it was valued at twenty-nine shillings per oz.

[2] In the *Portsmouth Gazette* of 1800 and 1801 are advertised such dress-goods as Shalloons, Russells, Calimancoes, Persians, Cypress gauzes, etc.

One cypress gown.
One striped Holland gown.
Two chintz gowns.
Two green Russell gowns.
One plaid Russell gown.
One black and blue Russell gown.
One homespun stuff gown.
One stuff gown.
One homespun cotton and linen gown.
One grosgrain skirt.
One black Calimanco skirt.
One silk quilted coat.
One Shalloon coat.
One cotton coat.
One black Shalloon coat.
One blue drugget coat.
One cotton and woollen coat.
Two waistcoats.
One drugget wrapper.
One silk shawl.
One velvet handkerchief.
One Holland handkerchief.
One Bilboa handkerchief.
One Barcelona handkerchief.[1]
One silk blanket.
Eight pair of gloves.

Besides ribbons, cambric aprons, Holland aprons, muslin aprons, silk stockings, China bed-curtains, chintz

---

[1] The silk handkerchiefs of Barcelona are famous to this day. The beautiful promenade of the *Rambla*, in that city, is brilliant on a holiday morning with these gay sheeny kerchiefs on the heads of the dark-eyed women. and every jaunty Catalonian, tripping along in his hemp *alpagartas*, has

"A new Barcelona tied round his *nate* neck,"

like the well known Irishman at Donnybrook fair.

bed-curtains, a silk quilt, household linen of all kinds, some silver utensils, an array of pewter, brass, and iron ware, silver money to the amount of more than £26, notes of hand, domestic animals, lands in her own right, etc., etc.

Mrs. Thompson, in her will, after suitable bequests to her children, gave her brother Solomon[1] her part of her father's share of the common lands in Durham, and her negro woman, Dinah. To her niece, Hannah, daughter of Micah Emerson, she gave a riding-hood that had belonged to her mother, Judith Emerson. This Hannah married William Allen. Among their descendants is the Hon. John D. Lyman, of Exeter. To the Rev. Joseph Prince she gave one cow, to be "well wintered" the year after her decease.[2]

---

[1] Solomon, son of Capt. Samuel Emerson, was a prominent man in Madbury. By the act of the incorporation of that town he was authorized to call the first town-meeting, which he did July 26, 1755, and was chosen moderator. For many years he was one of the selectmen and a justice of the peace.

[2] The Rev. Joseph Prince was at that time settled in Barrington, N. H., and often preached in Durham, where he seems to have been popular. He was totally blind from his fourteenth year, but having a retentive memory he prepared for the ministry, and was noted for his religious fervor. After many years he removed to Candia. He died at an advanced age in 1798, and was buried in Newburyport, in the same church as the celebrated Whitefield. He had twelve sons, popularly called in New Hampshire "The twelve Princes," who took turns in accompanying their blind father in his pastoral rounds. One of them was James, for many years collector of the customs at Newburyport. Another was Deacon Ezekiel Prince, who died Jan. 18, 1852, aged ninety-two.

Children of Robert and Abigail Thompson :

I. *Samuel.* Baptized in his infancy, March 22, 1723, by the Rev. Hugh Adams. Married, June 21, 1749, by the Rev. John Adams, to Susanna Reynolds, of Durham. Died before March 26, 1755, on which day his estate was admitted to probate. Being the oldest son, he received a double portion of his father's estate, including a farm called Camsoe,[1] along the banks of the Oyster river, where he established himself in a house on Mast road, —a thoroughfare opened in early times, leading to tide-water mark at Oyster River falls, for the purpose of conveying the choice pines destined for masts in the royal navy and other shipping of colonial days, which were sent down the river to Portsmouth. Samuel Thompson was not only engaged in agriculture, and in supplying lumber, but was interested in navigation, and owned a sloop,—per-

---

[1] Some have supposed Camsoe to be an Indian name, and a legend is still related in that neighborhood in support of this derivation ; but the farm originally belonged to Moses Davis, who was killed by the Indians, as above related, and the name is doubtless a corruption of Canseau or Canso, and a reminiscence of the campaigns to Port Royal, where he accompanied his brother, Col. James Davis, who took so prominent a part in them. I find this name given to the farm as early as April 14, 1723, when it was deeded to Robert Thompson. It has recently been sold by his descendants, and no longer bears the name ; but there is a spring in one of the fields, remarkable for the purity of its water, which is still known as "Camsoe spring."

haps "the good sloop Nancy," of which his enterprising mother bought a part after she became a
widow. A negro slave, named Sidon, is mentioned
in his inventory.

His only child, Hannah (b. July 29, 1749; d.
Dec. 25, 1841), married her cousin, Capt. Smith
Emerson, who was an efficient officer in the Revolutionary army, first stationed as captain, under
Col. Wingate, at Seavey's island, in the Piscataqua
harbor, Nov. 5, 1775.[1] He was afterwards captain
of Company Six, in Col. Tash's regiment, raised in
1776 to reinforce the continental army in New York.
His commission was signed by Washington himself,
under whom his regiment served, taking an active
part in the battles of White Plains, Trenton, and
Princeton, and, though suffering for want of clothing
in the severe weather of December and January,
1777, continued in service till March, six weeks after
its time had expired, contributing greatly to the suc-
cess of our army, and affording an admirable exam-
ple of courage and endurance that was exceptional,
even in those patriotic times. His son, Samuel
Emerson, died in the War of 1812–1815, at Sackett's
Harbor.

II. *Robert* (b. July 8, 1726; d. Jan. 12, 1805). He
married Susanna Thompson, and settled on his father's lands at Little River, in Lee, N. H., still owned

---

[1] "Adjt. General's Report of N. H. Regiments," II : 274.

by his descendants, most of whom have borne the quaint old names of Puritan times, such as Pelatiah, Jonathan, Deborah, etc. Robert Thompson seems to have been less patriotic than his surviving brother, for he refused to sign the Association test in 1776.

III. *Benjamin*, b. in 1731 ; d. Jan. 17, 173⅞.

IV. *Ebenezer*, b. March 5, 1737, O. S.; m. Mary Torr, May 22, 1758 ; d. Aug. 14, 1802. The principal subject of this memoir.

V. *Abigail*, b. June 23, 1747; d. April 15, 1816. She married Col. Timothy Emerson (brother of the above mentioned Capt. Smith Emerson), who was very efficient in raising troops during the Revolution, as shown by old papers still preserved by his descendants, as well as by public documents.

MEMOIR.

EBENEZER THOMPSON, the fourth child of the above
Robert and Abigail, was born March 5, 1737, O. S.
His father died when he was about fourteen years
of age, and although the youngest son, he succeeded
to the homestead estate, according to the "ultimo-
geniture" mode, then very common in New Hampshire, of giving the family place to the youngest son,
that he might remain at home and take care of his
parents in their old age. With his mother's acquies-
cence, he fell by degrees under the guidance of an
intimate friend of his father's, and an uncle by marriage.[1] This was Dr. Joseph Atkinson, a near relative of the Hon. Theodore Atkinson of Portsmouth,
so prominent in the affairs of New Hampshire before
the Revolution, and the owner, it is said, of one fifth
of the province. Dr. Atkinson came to Durham

---

[1] That is to say, a *quasi* uncle, Dr. Atkinson having married,
for his second wife, the widow of Col. Timothy Emerson, above
mentioned.

about the year 1734, and bought the Huckins farm, adjoining the land of Robert Thompson. Having no children of his own, he took a warm interest in his friend's youngest son, assumed the direction of his education, gave a bent to his mind, and finally made him his heir.[1] It was through his influence that Ebenezer Thompson studied medicine, of which he was a practitioner till he entered upon his political career. Hence he is often called " Dr. Thompson " in the early records and documents. I find his profession first mentioned in a deed of May 5, 1762, in which he is styled "Ebenezer Thompson, *physition*." He was then twenty-four years of age. But he never liked his profession, and finally abandoned it. Gov. Plumer says " he was esteemed a good physician, but as his talents qualified him for office the people required his service, and he yielded prompt obedience to their will."[2] This implies that he gave up the practice of medicine solely from patriotic motives, which perhaps was the case. The earliest town office he held was in March, 1765, when he was chosen one of the selectmen ; to which office he was annually reëlected for ten years, when other duties obliged him to relinquish it.

[1] Dr. Atkinson's slave, Scipio, served in Colonel Hercules Mooney's regiment, in 1758, under the name of "Sippo negro." N. H. State Papers, XIV : 21.

[2] Sketch of Judge Thompson, by Gov. William Plumer of Epping, still in MS.

February 6, 1766, he was chosen to represent the town of Durham at the General Assembly in Portsmouth, which he continued to do for ten years,—that is, till the Revolution. He soon became a prominent member of the house, and took a decided stand for the rights of the people. February 11, 1773, he was, with four others, empowered to administer to all officers of government, both civil and military, the oaths appointed by parliament, and "cause them to subscribe the test therein contained, together with the oath of abjuration." That same day he appeared before Theodore Atkinson, and took the oath of qualification.

At the council of May 10, 1773, he was appointed by Gov. Wentworth justice of the peace for Strafford county.

Among the important committees to which he belonged in the General Assembly, I find " Dr. Thompson," Dr. Josiah Bartlett, and two others, appointed in 1773, "to see what temporary laws had expired, or were near expiring, and consider what laws might be altered to advantage, and what new ones might be necessary." And from that time till his death, thirty years after, no change, as will be seen, was proposed in the laws or constitution of New Hampshire in which he did not have a voice.

At that time, it is said, " Dr. Bartlett, Dr. Thompson,[1] Col. Giddinge, and Col. Nathaniel Folsom, from Exeter, were the principal leaders in the house ;"[2] but though they all held commissions from the royal government, they were resolutely opposed to all encroachments on the rights of the people. Ebenezer Thompson's name has the signal honor of being connected with the very last act of the royal government in New Hampshire. This was in June, 1775, when the house of representatives voted not to receive three members from Grafton county, who had been "sent by virtue of the king's writ only," from towns which had not heretofore had that privilege, and without the concurrence of the other branches of the legislature. This was considered as "a breach of the spirit and design of the English constitution, and pregnant with alarming consequences."

This proceeding of the house drew a remonstrance from Gov. Wentworth, as an infringement on his majesty's prerogative and the rights of the people ; and he recommended to the house to rescind its vote and leave the three members free to take their seats.

That same day, July 14, 1775, the house voted that Capt. Langdon, Col. Bartlett, Dr. Thompson, and Meshech Weare be appointed to prepare an answer

---

[1] Dr. Thompson, by mistake, is said to be " of Dover."

[2] "Farmer and Moore's Hist. Coll.," I : 147.

to his excellency's message. Their reply, refusing to rescind the vote and giving the reasons, was so unsatisfactory to Gov. Wentworth that he immediately ordered the house to adjourn. This was July 15, 1775, and the General Assembly of the Provincial Government never met again.[1]

Meanwhile, meetings were held by the leaders of the opposition, and a correspondence entered into with Massachusetts and other provinces by means of a committee to which Ebenezer Thompson belonged. Between July 21, 1774, and Jan. 5, 1776, five conventions, called " congresses," were held in Exeter, all of which Ebenezer Thompson attended as delegate from Durham, acting as secretary. And a general congress of all the colonies was called that year, to meet in Philadelphia, in order to concert future measures.

In the town records of Durham is the following entry, under the date of July 18, 1774: " Voted that two persons attend at Exeter with full powers to join in the choice of delegates to attend at the General Congress to be held at Philadelphia on the first day of Sept. next. Ebenezer Thompson, Esq., chosen to attend as aforesaid, and John Sullivan, Esq., the other." The same day it was voted "that the selectmen pay the sum of 4£, 10s, out of the town stock for the purpose of paying the delegates." And Jan.

[1] N. H. State Papers, VIII : 383–386.

2, 1775, they were again both chosen as deputies to Exeter, with full power to act in the choice of delegates to the intended congress, to be held at Philadelphia on the 10th of May following.

But there is one important act in which Ebenezer Thompson took part that has been passed over. This was the seizure of Fort William and Mary, at New Castle,—the first open act of the Revolution in New Hampshire,—which took place Dec. 14, 1774, four months before the skirmish at Lexington. The chief honor of this has generally been attributed to Gen. Sullivan, then a major in the New Hampshire militia, and a practitioner of law in Durham. It seems, however, to have been a widely concerted plan, in which prominent representative men from the chief towns in the province took part, such as John Langdon of Portsmouth, Josiah Bartlett of Kingston, Nathaniel Peabody of Plaistow, Nicholas Gilman, Nathaniel Folsom, and Dr. Giddinge of Exeter, etc.

The party that went from Durham consisted of about thirteen men, among whom were Major Sullivan and one of his brothers, Ebenezer Thompson, John Griffin, and Lieut. Winborn Adams. Capt. John Demerit also went with them to represent the town of Madbury. Alexander Scammell, afterwards a general in the Revolutionary army, and mortally wounded at Yorktown, is said by some to have

accompanied them, but his name is not mentioned
in the account of the expedition given by Eleazar
Bennet of Durham, who was also a member of it.[1]
Of this party Major Sullivan was undoubtedly the
leader.[2] They went down the Oyster and Piscataqua
rivers in the night of December 13, in an open
freight-boat, called in this region a " gundalow."
At Portsmouth they joined a much larger party.
The Hon. Woodbury Langdon, in a cautious letter
of Dec. 17, 1774, says,—" Some hundreds, if not
thousands, of men went to the fort, as it is said,

[1] Mr. Bennet's account, related when he was about 100 years
of age, was written down by the Rev. Alvan Tobey of Durham. and published in the *Congregational Journal* of February, 1852.

[2] Of the above mentioned party, *Winborn Adams* (grandson
of the Rev. Hugh Adams, the first settled minister at Oyster
River), was at that time an inn-holder in Durham, as was his
widow after him. At the beginning of the Revolutionary war
he was commissioned to raise a company in Durham, of which
he was appointed captain. He proved a brave officer, and had
attained to the rank of lieutenant-colonel, when he was killed at
the battle of Bemis Heights, in 1777.

John Griffin was appointed first lieutenant under Capt.
Adams in 1775.

Capt. John Demerit, a kinsman of the present writer, was
at that time just fifty years of age, and the leading man in Madbury. He was an extensive land-owner, and for many years
one of the selectmen. He was also a justice of the peace, and
a captain in the New Hampshire militia. In 1776 and 1777 he
represented the town of Madbury in the General Assembly at
Exeter. As will be seen further on, he received the appointment of major for his services to the province.

and have taken thence all the Arms and Powder, fearing the King's Troops might deprive the province of their Arms, Ammunition, etc., as has been reported is intended. What the result of this, no man can tell."[1]

The greater part of these people must have gone merely to testify their approval and witness the capture, for the fort was in a ruinous condition, and only defended by Col. Cochran and five men. But the leaders required, and must have had, great moral courage to commit a deliberate, overt act of defiance against Great Britain ; and therein lay the heroism of the deed. Mr. Brewster, in his " Rambles about Portsmouth," says this expedition was first planned by Capt. Thomas Pickering,[2] of that town, and that he was the real leader. At all events, he was the first to scale the walls of the fort, and to him Col. Cochran, the commander, surrendered his sword.[3]

---

[1] Letter to Webster and Eastman. " New England Hist. and Gen. Register."

[2] The Adjutant-General's Report of New Hampshire Regiments says the band was " under the command" of Capt. Pickering. Mr. Amory, in his Life of Gen. Sullivan, says Sullivan " planned the attack with Thomas Pickering and John Langdon," which seems probable.

Capt. Pickering, a kinsman of the present writer, was then only about thirty years of age. He was the son of Capt. Thos. Pickering, a brave officer, who in the expedition to Casco bay in 1746 was taken by the Indians and literally sliced in pieces.

[3] This is a tradition handed down in the family.

The arms and ammunition of the fort were carried for safety into the interior, and distributed among different towns.[1] A large part of the powder was brought to Durham, and at first concealed under the meeting-house,[2] which stood on a high bank overlooking the Oyster river; but it was soon removed to a less accessible place in Madbury, where Capt. Demerit had an underground magazine built for it, leading from his own cellar.[3]

In the Fourth Provincial Congress at Exeter, a vote of thanks was given to "the persons who took away and secured for the use of the Province the gunpowder in the fort of William and Mary." And Nov. 9, 1775, it was voted "that Capt. John Demerit be first Major of the Second Regiment of militia in this colony," no doubt in recognition of his services in this affair.[4]

---

[1] See the letter of Aug. 7, 1775, from the Committee of Safety to Major Cilley (New Hampshire Provincial Papers, VII: 573), desiring him "to apply to the selectmen of the *several towns* in this colony with whom was lodged the Powder taken last winter from Fort William and Mary * * and request them to convey the whole of it to Col. Nicholas Gilman of Exeter."

[2] This meeting-house, which stood nearly opposite the inn of Winborn Adams, was taken down in 1792.

[3] This powder was afterwards sent to Bunker Hill and Cambridge, by the special order of Gen. Washington and Gen. Sullivan. Capt. Demerit reserved some of it for the use of his own regiment, and his descendants still show with pride a powder-horn containing a small portion.

[4] See N. H. Prov. Papers, VII: 655.

Gov. Wentworth declared the offenders guilty of treason, and called upon the public to deliver them up to justice ; probably as a mere matter of form, for he must have seen how useless it was to attempt reprisals for so popular a movement. I have, however, seen it stated more than once that he dismissed Majors Langdon and Sullivan from their command in the militia, and deprived Josiah Bartlett and Ebenezer Thompson of their commissions as justices of the peace, as if he regarded them as prominent leaders in the affair.[1]

---

[1] The following letter from Gov. Wentworth has come to light since the above was written, among the papers received from Halifax last year (1885), and seems to bear on the question whether any proceedings were taken against Ebenezer Thompson, in particular, for the part he took in the capture of Fort William and Mary. As he, and not Major Sullivan, was at that time the most prominent man in civil affairs in Durham,[1] his joining the expedition has special significance, and proves him to have been one of the leaders of the Durham party.

" Portsmouth, March 15, 1775.
" To Theophilus Dame, Esq., Sheriff of Strafford County in the Province of New Hampshire :

" Sir : A writ of supersedeas vs. Ebenezer Thompson, Esq[r] having passed & by my order to be transmitted to you, I hereby direct that the service of said writ be suspended until further orders from me.

" I am, Sir, your most humble servant,
" J. W."

[1] Mr. Amory says that Major Sullivan was a member of the Provincial Assembly in the spring of 1774 (see his Life of Gen. Sullivan, page 10), but this is a mistake. The representative from Durham was Ebenezer Thompson.

Mr. Amory, in his Life of Gen. Sullivan, says the party from Durham showed their defiance by assembling at the tavern of Winborn Adams and marching in procession to the neighboring common, near the meeting-house, where, in the presence of a large crowd, all who held royal commissions burnt them, and all insignia of office connecting them in any way with the royal government. A bonfire on this height would be seen to a great distance, especially down the valley of the Oyster river.

However this may be, Ebenezer Thompson certainly continued to fulfil his duties under royal commission as late as April 15, 1775. I do not, to be sure, find his commission of justice of the peace, but I have in my possession the before mentioned commission of Feb. 11, 1773, authorizing him and four others, among whom is Gen. Sullivan, to administer the oaths appointed by parliament to all officers of government, both civil and military. And I have another commission of April 15, 1775, signed also by Gov. Wentworth, appointing Henry Rust and Joseph Sias, Esquires, special justices of the Inferior Court of Common Pleas, then sitting at Durham, to which is appended the attestation that the same day the said Henry Rust and Joseph Sias appeared and took the aforesaid oaths before John Wentworth (of Dover) and Ebenezer Thompson, commissioners.[1]

[1] Gen. Sullivan was then at Philadelphia.

At the opening of the Second Provincial Congress at Exeter, Jan. 25, 1775, Ebenezer Thompson was, by vote of the delegates, chosen one of a committee of seven with power "to call a Provincial Convention of deputies when they shall judge the exigencies of public affairs shall require it."[1] When news came, the following April, of the battle of Lexington, this committee hastened to meet at Durham, where Ebenezer Thompson resided, to call a convention at once. Alexander Scammell, in a letter to Gen. Sullivan, who was then in Philadelphia, says,—" I went express for Boston by desire of the Congressional Committee, then (April 20) sitting at Durham; proceeded as far as Bradford, where I obtained credible information that evening, and next morning arrived at Exeter where the Provincial Congress was assembling with all possible haste."[2]

That same day, April 20, a town-meeting was held in Durham, and Ebenezer Thompson, with three other deputies, was chosen " to attend the Provincial Council at Exeter *forthwith*." The next day sixty-six members arrived at Exeter to consider " what measures would be most expedient at this alarming crisis." Ebenezer Thompson was chosen clerk of the convention,[3] and that same day was appointed one of the

[1] N. H. Prov. Papers, VII : 442.
[2] Mr. Amory's " Life of Gen. Sullivan," p. 299.
[3] N. H. Prov. Papers, VII : 454.

committee to reply to the Massachusetts congress about the needs of the country.

During the Fourth Provincial Congress, at Exeter, in 1775, the Hon. Theodore Atkinson, former secretary of the province, by an order of the convention, as Belknap relates, "delivered up the Provincial records to a committee which was sent to receive them, and Ebenezer Thompson, Esq., was appointed in his place." And after the formation of a state government he was the first to hold the office of secretary of the state of New Hampshire,[1] and every succeeding year he was reäppointed by the legislature till June, 1786,—eleven years in all. He was also clerk of the senate from 1776 till 1786.

It was in this Fourth Congress that the Committee of Safety was first instituted in New Hampshire. The appointment of the members was considered the most important civil trust in the gift of the house, and none were chosen but men of unquestionable patriotism and integrity. All through the war it provided supplies for the army, and during the recesses of the assembly it acted as the supreme executive, and was sometimes called in consequence "The Little Congress." To this important body Ebenezer Thompson belonged during the most critical period

---

[1] The present secretary of the state of New Hampshire, Hon. A. B. Thompson, is the descendant of one of the Durham Thompsons, who removed to Holderness about the year 1770.

of the Revolution,—that is, from 1775 till 1781, when the war was virtually over. The number first appointed, May 20, 1775, only consisted of Josiah Bartlett, Matthew Thornton, Nathaniel Folsom, Ebenezer Thompson, and William Whipple; but the number was afterwards increased, and varied from year to year. Ebenezer Thompson was always secretary of this committee while he belonged to it, and frequently chairman *pro tem.* At the same time he belonged, in Durham, to the town Committee of Safety, of Correspondence, and of Inspection.

December 11, 1775, the town of Durham, in anticipation of a state form of government, chose Ebenezer Thompson representative for one year, "to act either as member of the Congress, or of such a government as should be assumed by a recommendation from the Continental Congress as would require a house of representatives." [1]

The second day of the Fifth Congress at Exeter, Dec. 22, 1775, Benjamin Giles, Ebenezer Thompson, and Wyseman Claggett, Esquires, were chosen a committee "to draw up a Solemn Obligation or Engagement to be entered into by the members of this Congress." [2]

December 27, 1775, Ebenezer Thompson was one of the persons appointed "to draw up a plan for the

---

[1] Town Records of Durham.
[2] N. H. Prov. Papers, VII : 693.

government of the Colony of N. H. during the con-
test with Great Britain;" on the 28th he was one of
the five men chosen "to form the plan of a constitution for the rule and government of the Colony,"
upon which business they were to enter "immediately;" and Jan. 9, 1776, he was chosen one of a
committee of six "to revise the system of laws lately
in force in this Colony, and to report what altera-
tions, additions, and amendments are necessary to be
made in our present circumstances for the guidance
of the executive officers of government."[1]

Under the temporary form of government established in 1776, New Hampshire took the name of a
"Colony."[2] The first meeting of the representatives
was held at Exeter Jan. 5, and that same day it was
voted "that Ebenezer Thompson, Esq[r], be Clerk of
this House."[3] The next day (January 6) he was appointed by vote of the house one of the twelve executive Councillors of New Hampshire,[4] which office he
held five years,—that is, till 1781. These Councillors
of State were chosen from "respectable freeholders
and inhabitants within the colony," and constituted
a kind of senatorial body, which, together with the

[1] N. H. Prov. Papers, VII : 703, 704, and Vol. VIII : 9.

[2] New Hampshire did not take the name of a "State" till
Sept. 10, 1776.

[3] N. H. State Papers, VIII : 5.

[4] N. H. State Papers, VIII : 6.

1762950

house of representatives, governed the state for several years. A president was chosen from their number, and any seven of them formed a quorum to do business.

January 26, 1776, Ebenezer Thompson, together with all the members of the council, was appointed justice of the peace and of the quorum throughout the colony.

The following items from the State Papers show what remuneration Ebenezer Thompson received in the various offices he held:

January 27, 1776. " Voted that Mr. Secretary Thompson shall receive Three Shillings per day for sixteen days' attendance on the late Congress as Secretary, over and above his wages (*sic*) as a member of said Congress, and that he receive Six Shillings per day for his services as Secretary to the Colony, over and above his wages as a Councillor."

February 10, 1776, nine shillings per day were voted to the Committee of Safety in the recess of the General Court, they paying their own expenses. They were allowed, however, the same sum for travel (two pence a mile) as the members of the house.

March 22, " The Com. of Safety allowed 8*s*. per day, they paying their own expenses."

September 20. " Pay of Council 6*s*. per day, and 2*d*. a mile for travel." " Com. of Safety 7*s*. per day, and travel." " Ebenezer Thompson, Sec^y, 6*s*. per day extra."

July 19, 1777. "Voted that the Honble Eben^r Thompson, Sec^y, be paid 6s. per day for his services in the Committee of Safety: also 6s. pr. day, the present sessions, over and above his pay as Councillor."

Two years later, after the currency had greatly depreciated, the members of the council received $5 per day; the Committee of Safety, in recess of assembly, $6; the secretary, for extra services, $5.

The first issue of paper currency in New Hampshire during the Revolutionary period was made under the direction of Ebenezer Thompson and Nicholas Gilman, who were appointed June 9, 1775, to "procure the plates and have struck off" notes of different values to the amount of £10,050. These notes bore their initials in the lower corners. The formula was as follows:[1]

Colony of New Hampshire.   July 25, 1775.
    The possessor of this Note shall be entitled of the Treasurer of this Colony, the Sum of * * * * Lawfull money, on the 20th Decr 1779, & this Note shall be received in all payments at the Treasury at any time after the date hereof.
    E. T.   N. G.

July 6, 1775, the receiver-general was ordered to "pay Eben^r Thompson, Esqr thirty-one pounds, four shillings, being the expense of making the £10,050,

[1] N. H. State Papers, VIII: 550.

lately emitted by order of the Congress of this Colony."[1]

June 4, 1776, Ebenezer Thompson received a commission as one of the justices "appointed by the Government and People of the Colony of N. H. to keep the Peace in the County of Strafford," signed by Meshech Weare, President of the Council, and bearing the seal of the Colony; which document is in the possession of the present writer.

During this period Ebenezer Thompson was repeatedly commissioned to transact public business in various places, as appears from the Records of the Committee of Safety. I quote a few instances:

August 1, 1775. "Col. Thornton, Dr. Bartlett, and Dr. Thompson, who, at the request of this Committee, went on Monday last (July 24) to confer with Gen¹ Washington and the Gen¹ Court of Mass³, returned on Friday evening, having been on that business five Days."

May 21, 1777. "Ordered the Rec' Gen. to pay Eben' Thompson 10s. for his expenses for horse hire, and Col. Bartlett's expenses, to Hawke, examining Paul Hale."[2]

---

[1] Records of the Committee of Safety.

[2] Hawke, now Danville. Paul Hale had been arrested for counterfeiting gold coin, but escaped further prosecution by becoming "State's evidence" against other coiners in New Hampshire and Massachusetts.

August 2, 1777. "Ordered the Rec. Gen. to pay Eben' Thompson £1–6s.–6d. for the expenses and horse hire for himself and Mr. Wentworth to Portsmouth on public business."

May 6, 1778. "Ordered the Rec' Gen. to pay Eben' Thompson £7–15s. for a journey to Holderness on public business."

January 2, 1778, Ebenezer Thompson and Nathaniel Peabody were appointed commissioners to New Haven to meet delegates from other states for the purpose of deciding some questions of national economy, such as the regulation of prices, then daily rising in consequence of the rapid depreciation of the currency.

In the celebrated controversy about the "New Hampshire grants," Ebenezer Thompson was appointed agent of the state to confer with a committee sent to that territory by the continental congress. The New Hampshire grants were so called from a great number of townships (there were 138 as early as 1763) west of the Connecticut river, granted by Gov. Benning Wentworth, who seems to have inferred from the royal instructions that this region fell within his jurisdiction. His grants were declared invalid by New York, which state claimed the whole territory, on the ground that it was included in a grant of Charles II to his brother, the Duke of York. The settlers themselves did not wish to belong to either state. They asked to be recognized as a separate state, and to be admitted into the federal union under the name of Vermont. This led to a bitter controversy with New York, whose influence prevented it for many years. New Hampshire took no special part in the dispute till sixteen towns along the eastern shore of the Connecticut river revolted against her authority, wishing either to unite with Vermont, which was disposed to receive them, or, in union with some towns on the western side of the river, to form a small state by themselves, declaring that, according to Mason's grant, the state of New Hampshire only extended back sixty miles from the sea, and did not include their territory. But the New Hampshire government firmly opposed any secession. In 1778 a committee was chosen, to which Ebenezer Thompson belonged, to draw up a remonstrance to the congress at Philadelphia against the proceedings of Vermont in " taking into union a certain number of towns on the N. H. frontier, and inviting others to revolt from the state, as an infringement on the confederacy of the United States, and the special rights of N. H.," and desiring congress to grant some order thereon " to prevent effusion of blood." June 26, 1779, it was voted[1]

---

[1] " June 26th, 1779, ordered the R. G. to Lett Ebenezer Thompson, Esqr, have one hundred and fifty pounds towards his Expences to the N. H. Grants, he to be accountable."

Records of the N. H. Committee of Safety.

"that the Hon[ble] Ebenezer Thompson, Esq[r] be, and
hereby is, chosen and appointed in behalf of this
state to repair to the N. H. Grants, and that he
be instructed to confer with the Committee of Congress, and lay before it the nature and origin of the
difficulty, and the action of the General Assembly,
and to answer any matters touching the dispute."[1]
The matter was finally referred to congress, which,
Aug. 20, 1781, declared to Vermont that it would be
an indispensable preliminary to her admission into
the Union to renounce all jurisdiction east of the
Connecticut river. To this, after some opposition,
consent was finally given ; but the dispute with New
York was not settled till 1791, when, on the 18th of
February, Vermont was, with the consent of all the
states, admitted into the Union.

It has been justly remarked, by one who is thor-
oughly acquainted with the records of New Hampshire,[2] that Ebenezer Thompson "was appointed on
more legislative committees to inquire into and report
on matters of dispute between towns, etc., than any
of his contemporaries, especially committees which
were authorized to sit when the legislature was not
in session."

Between 1780 and 1784, Ebenezer Thompson and
four others were appointed to lay out and settle the

---

[1] State Papers, X : 344.

[2] Isaac W. Hammond, Esq.

boundaries of Rumney, Wentworth, Warren, Plymouth, Campton, Piermont, and Orford, and their report was declared "binding and conclusive in law upon all persons and parties whatsoever."[1] Nor were these the only towns whose limits he helped decide. As early as 1768 he settled, with the aid of two others, the line between Hampton and Hampton Falls, and in 1770 the line between South Hampton and Newtown.[2] In early life he was an authorized land-surveyor, a profession which ranked with the civil engineer of the present day. And he was a good draughtsman. He drew the plan of the church built in Durham in 1792,[3] a fine specimen of the genuine New England meeting-house,—lofty, spacious, and well lighted; with broad galleries around three sides, a monumental pulpit high up at the east end, and surmounted by a sounding-board suspended from the roof. Beneath was a solemn "deacons' seat," facing the whole congregation, who were seated in square roomy pews in six tiers, two of which stood higher up against the walls, as if of more aristocratic pretensions. At the west end was a square tower with a tall spire visible to a great extent, where hung a fine-toned bell that could be heard at the

[1] N. H. State Papers, XI:729–731.

[2] Now called Newton.

[3] The town records speak of the plan of this meeting-house as made by Noah Jewett, but it was doubtless drawn for him by Judge Thompson, according to a record in the family.

very mouth of the Oyster river. This interesting
building, which stood on the spot where the historic gunpowder had first been secreted in 1774,
was taken down in 1848, and the materials sold to
build tenement houses in a neighboring manufac-
turing town.

But to return to Revolutionary times. At the
town-meeting in Durham, April 2, 1778, it was voted "that the Honble Ebenezer Thompson, Esqr, Be,
and is hereby, Appointed to attend the Convention
at Concord—for the forming and laying a permanent
plan or system of government for the future happi-
ness and well-being of the people of the state, and
to pass any vote or votes relative thereto that may
be deemed expedient." He accepted the office, and
was the delegate from Durham in 1778 and 1779,
and was chosen secretary of the convention.

August 14, 1778, he was appointed one of the
representatives of New Hampshire to the Continental Congress at Philadelphia for one year; but he
declined the appointment.[1] He was always averse
to any prolonged absence from home because of his
general feebleness of health, and, in particular, an
affection of the heart that finally caused his death.
It was undoubtedly this reason which made him
relinquish part of his offices in 1781.

February 27, 1783, he was again chosen to rep-

[1] N. H. State Papers, VIII: 789.

resent the State of New Hampshire in Congress; but he again declined the honor.[1]

August 20, 1778, he was appointed Special Justice of the Superior Court,[2] but this must have been for a short time, or on some particular occasion, for he does not appear to have retained the office.

June 14, 1783, he was appointed Justice of the Superior Court of Judicature, in place of the Hon. Woodbury Langdon, who had resigned;[3] but he did not accept the position.

Holding, as he did, all through the most critical period of the Revolution, the three important offices of Councillor of State, member of the Committee of Safety, and Secretary of the State, besides minor offices of town and court, and various public commissions, it will be seen that Ebenezer Thompson was by no means an inactive statesman. After the organization of the courts of law under the constitution of the state in 1783, he was appointed clerk of the Court of Common Pleas in the county of Strafford, which office he held till September, 1787, when it was given to his son Benjamin. In 1786 and 1787 he was the representative of Durham at the General Assembly. He was again chosen member of the executive council in 1787 for one year; and state

---

[1] N. H. State Papers, VIII : 969.

[2] N. H. State Papers, VIII : 792.

[3] N. H. State Papers, VIII : 977.

senator in 1787 and 1788. On the 7th of September, 1787, he was appointed Justice of the Inferior Court of Common Pleas in Strafford county, which office he held till April 3, 1795, when he accepted the appointment of Justice of the Superior Court of Judicature. Gov. Plumer says " this office required so much time and travel that it fatigued him, and in the spring of 1796 he resigned it." [1]

In a brief notice of Judge Thompson, published in the *N. H. Gazette* in 1802, it says he filled the office of Judge of the Superior Court " with great credit ;" but " his advanced life would not admit of his travelling the circuit, and he resigned. After this he was prevailed upon to accept the office of Judge of the Court of Common Pleas for the county of Strafford, which did not require him to go far from home." This last reäppointment was made May 12, 1796, and he held the office till his death in 1802. Altogether, he was a judge for more than fifteen years.

During all this time he held many town offices in Durham, among which was that of town-clerk, which he held from 1765 till 1774, with the exception of one year, and from 1793 till 1801—in all, eighteen years. After being for several years one of the selectmen, he was assessor of taxes, and commissioner and auditor of accounts, and was on most of the committees for the interests of the parish. In

[1] Gov. William Plumer's MS.

1784 I find him and Gen. Sullivan both overseers of the poor. At the town-meeting in Durham in 1788, it was voted "that the hon^ble Ebenezer Thompson, Esq., and His Excellency John Sullivan, Esq., be assessors and commissioners," at which time the latter was president of the state, and the former Judge of the C. C. P. And both were at different times among the committee of the district schools.

It has sometimes been said that Judge Thompson was a lawyer by profession; but, strictly speaking, he was not, though consulted as one by people from all parts of the state. He never opened an office, and always gave his advice gratis. It was in one of these consultations that he spent the last hours of his laborious life.

Judge Thompson had the honor of belonging to the college of Presidential Electors of New Hampshire when George Washington was first chosen President of the United States, and was likewise appointed to that trust at the three following elections of 1792, 1796, and 1800, giving his vote for Washington and Adams, and afterwards for Adams and Ellsworth, and Adams and Pinckney.

He was also a member of the convention held in Concord in 1791–1792 for the purpose of revising the constitution of the state, and, as Gov. Plumer remarks, "took an active and efficient part in that business." He was here appointed one of the com-

mittee to prepare a draught of "such amendments
as should be thought necessary to be sent out to the
people." When the question was put to vote whether
the clause that the civil officers of the state "shall be
of the Protestant religion" should be struck out of
the constitution or not, Judge Thompson voted in
the affirmative, together with many other statesmen
of liberal and enlightened views, such as William
Plumer of Epping, Jeremiah Smith of Peterborough,
Nathaniel Peabody of Atkinson, etc. But the nega-
tives carried the day, and this clause remained the
test of office till 1876.

Judge Thompson was so popular in his native
county of Strafford that in 1794 he received 846
votes as governor, in opposition to John Taylor
Gilman; and in the Durham records of that year is
the following item: "Votes for a Governor were
called for, taken, sorted, and counted, and it appeared that there were for Eben' Thompson, Esq.
178; for John T. Gilman, Esq. 10."

The testimony of Gov. Plumer concerning the
character and ability of Judge Thompson, coming
from a contemporary and personal friend, is too
valuable to be omitted. He says,—"From a long
and intimate acquaintance with him I know he was a
man of much reading and general information. His
manners were simple, plain, and unassuming. He
had a strong aversion to extravagance and parade

of every kind. *Usefulness* was the object of all his pursuits, both in relation to himself and the public. Though he never exhibited a passion for wealth, yet by his frugality and economy he supported his family and left them a handsome estate. He was a man of sound judgment, of a clear, discriminating mind, retentive memory, and great decision of character. He was distinguished for perseverance, and never abandoned his pursuit so long as he saw a prospect of attaining his object. He was cautious and prudent, shrewd and cunning, and distrusted men whom he did not know. . . Those who knew him best considered him upright and honest. . . As a legislator, he was industrious, efficient, and useful. Though he was not an eloquent or graceful speaker, his arguments were clear and logical, concise and confined to the subject; and his influence in popular assemblies was great. In party politics he was a steady, undeviating Federalist.

"As Secretary of the State, he was attentive and faithful to his trust. Though he was not a lawyer, yet as a judge he appeared to advantage. He knew the character of almost every man in the county in which he lived, and his decisions were just and equitable. And, as it respected the prudential concerns of the county, no man could more effectually promote its interest."[1]

---

[1] Gov. William Plumer's MS.

48

Judge Thompson died suddenly Aug. 14, 1802, in the 65th year of his age. After dining at home with a gentleman from a neighboring town, who had come to consult him on some point of law, he withdrew with his client to the so-called " hall-room," and soon after, while sitting there, book in hand, he fell from his chair and instantly expired.

His five children were at this time all married; and he had five grandsons, all bearing the name of Ebenezer,—one of the homely Old Testament names to which New Englanders were partial, but which he rendered so dear to the family that it has been perpetuated in it to this day, every generation thus far having had an Ebenezer. Each of these five grandsons is mentioned by name in the first draught of his will.

The estate he left his children chiefly consisted of large tracts of land, comprising the homestead and Atkinson farms in Durham, a farm and other lands in Lee, wood lands in Barrington, one fourteenth part of the town of Maynesborough[1] (about 2,200 acres), and 1,400 acres in Peeling,[2] of which he was one of

---

[1] Maynesborough, now Berlin, Coös county, N. H., was first granted in 1771 to Sir William Mayne and others of Barbadoes.

[2] The township of Peeling, now Woodstock, was first granted Sept. 23, 1763, to Eli Demerit of Madbury, but the grant having apparently been forfeited by non-settlement, " Dr. Thompson, Esq' of Durham " petitioned in 1771 for a new charter, which was granted by Gov. John Wentworth Nov. 24, 1771, " to the subscribers in such proportions as they subscribe for." Dr. Thompson took 1,400 acres.

the original grantees,—about 4,000 acres in all. I find in the *N. H. Gazette*, of April 7, 1801, Ebenezer Thompson, William K. Atkinson of Dover, Benjamin Barron, and Thomas Coggswell mentioned as owners of more than one sixteenth part of Lincoln in Grafton county.

Judge Thompson's wife was Mary, daughter of Vincent Torr, a native of Devonshire, England, who about 1740 came over to be the heir of his uncle, Benedictus Torr of Dover. The family in England were apparently people of substance. Simon, the brother of Mrs. Thompson, made in early life a visit to his relatives beyond the sea; and a wealthy aunt near London offered to give him her property if he would remain in that country. But, chiefly through the influence of Judge Thompson, it is said, he renounced the idea; and finally settled in Rochester, where he amassed a handsome fortune, and where his descendants still live.[1]

Mrs. Thompson, on the maternal side, was a lineal descendant of Richard Otis of Dover, and of his first wife, who, according to the " Otis Genealogy," was

---

[1] Among Simon Torr's grandchildren are John McDuffee, Esq., to whom the town of Rochester owes so much of its prosperity; John F. Torr, Esq., the present county commissioner; and the late John Brewster, banker, of Boston, who left nearly $2,000,000, part of which he bequeathed to endow a free school and build a public library at Wolfeborough, N. H., and for other benefactions in that town and in Tuftonborough.

Rose Stoughton, the sister of Sir Nicholas Stough-
ton of England, baronet, and a near relative of Col.
Israel and Gov. William Stoughton of Massachusetts.
Her father, Anthony Stoughton, was an inflexible
Roundhead of Cromwell's time, and served in the
Parliamentary army. The uncertain condition of
England, and his approaching end, induced him
to confide his daughter to Col. Israel Stoughton,
who brought her to New England, then a genuine land of promise to the Puritans. Here she
married Richard Otis, one of the early pioneers of
New Hampshire, and of a family that has illustrated
more than one commonwealth by statesmen, magis-
trates, and useful citizens of various other grades.
He came to New Hampshire about the year 1656,
and settled in Dover, where he had a grant of land.
Here he built a garrison and erected a forge,—the
first, or one of the first, in the settlement. A few
years later he was one of the selectmen. He under-
stood surveying, so necessary an acquirement to the
pioneer, and is frequently spoken of as " laying out
land." In 1669 he helped settle the boundaries
between Exeter and Lamprey River (Newmarket.)
In March, 16⅞, he was appointed the agent of
Robert Mason, " lord proprietor of the Province of
New Hampshire," with power to collect rents, and
prevent trespasses of all kinds on his lands in
Dover, Cocheco, Newichwannock, Oyster River, etc.

It was this Richard Otis whose garrison was burned in 1689 by the Indians, who killed him and his son Stephen and his daughter Hannah, and carried the rest of the family into captivity. A part of them were rescued a few days after,—among them his daughter Rose and her brother Nicholas (a namesake of his uncle, Sir Nicholas Stoughton), who was afterwards killed by the Indians July 26, 1696,—but the others, including Mrs. Otis (a third wife) and her infant daughter Christine, were carried to Canada. The latter became noted for her romantic history. She was educated in a convent, and brought up in the Catholic faith. At an early age she married M. Le Beau, a Frenchman, who died a few years after, leaving her a young, attractive widow. In 1713 she captivated Capt. Thomas Baker, one of the commissioners to Canada for the redemption of captives,—a brave, adventurous man, chiefly known for a successful attack on the Indians in the Pemigewasset valley, near the mouth of the stream since called " Baker's river." It was with great difficulty that the release of Christine Le Beau was effected ; but Capt. Baker finally overcame all the obstacles presented by the authorities, induced her to abandon her children, her mother, and her religion, and bore her off triumphantly to New England. Perhaps at a later day she was convinced that the *jeu ne valait pas la chandelle*, for after many vicissitudes she was

obliged to open an inn in Dover for her own main-
tenance and to support him in his old age. This
Christine Baker was the half-sister of Rose Otis, the
great-grandmother of Mary Torr, who became the
wife of Judge Thompson.

Mary Torr was born Sept. 1, 1740, O. S. She
married Ebenezer Thompson May 22, 1758. They
had five children, viz.,—

I. *Sarah*, b. Feb. 16, 1759; d. Jan. 16, 1807. As
early as 1777 she married James Laighton, a descendant of Thomas Layton, one of the signers of
the "combination for government" at Dover, N. H.,
in 1640, and a freeman and selectman in 1658.
James Laighton in early life served under the celebrated Com. John Paul Jones. Of him and his wife
Sarah there are numerous descendants.

II. *Ann*, b. Jan. 30, 1761; d. Oct. 11, 1829. She
married, Feb. 22, 1781, the Rev. Curtis Coe, then
pastor of the Congregational church in Durham,
and the last minister who was settled here by the
town authorities. He descended from Robert Coe,
a native of Suffolkshire, England, who came to
America in 1634. The Rev. Curtis Coe was born
in Middletown, Conn., July 21, 1750; graduated at
Brown University in 1776; and ordained in Durham Nov. 1, 1780. He resigned his pastorate
May 1, 1805, and became a home missionary in the
remote parts of New Hampshire and Maine. He

died in New Market, N. H., June 7, 1829, leaving many descendants.

III. *Ebenezer*, b. July 12, 1762; d. Feb. 4, 1828. He was generally called "Col. Thompson," having received, June 18, 1799, the commission of Lieutenant-Colonel of the 25th N. H. Regiment. He was an enterprising man, and very early in life engaged in home and foreign trade, and in ship-building at Durham, in which he was so successful that in the year 1800 he was the largest tax-payer in the town, being already much wealthier than his father. His fortunes were still more improved by his removal in 1803 to Portsmouth, where he acquired considerable real estate, and had ships at sea. A few years later he met with severe reverses through the "embargo," and the "great fire" of 1813, in which he lost $40,000 in one night. He was a man of brilliant parts, and might have distinguished himself in political life or at the bar. He was a fluent speaker, and used to plead his own cases in court. According to the town records of Durham, he had, July 8, 1793, ninety-seven votes (against twenty-four for Jonathan Steele, Esq., afterwards Judge—the son-in-law of Gen. Sullivan) as representative to the legislature, and for the next six years he was reëlected to the same office, sometimes unanimously, and at other times by a very large majority. And he was at that time Justice of the Peace.

Col. Thompson was married three times. His first wife was Martha Burleigh of New Market, N. H., a descendant of two of the early governors of Massachusetts, her mother being the granddaughter of Col. Winthrop Hilton, whose great-grandmother was Ann Dudley, the granddaughter both of Gov. John Winthrop and of Gov. Thomas Dudley. She died in 1796, and lies buried with one of her children in the Durham church-yard.

Col. Thompson's second wife was Mary, daughter of William and Eleanor (March) Weeks, of one of the most respectable families in Greenland, N. H. From them have sprung a large, and for the most part prosperous, family.

Col. Thompson's third wife was Elizabeth Hale, daughter of Major Samuel Hale, an officer in the expedition against Louisbourg in 1745, and afterwards, for nearly forty years, Master of the Latin Grammar School in Portsmouth, N. H. She left no children.

IV. *Benjamin*, b. March 31, 1765; d. Jan. 21, 1838. He married, May 11, 1794, Mary Pickering of Newington (b. June 15, 1774; d. Oct. 1 1849), a descendant of John Pickering,[1] one of the early

---

[1] See the "Pickering Genealogy," compiled by R. H. Eddy, Esq., of Boston, Mass., whose wife is a great-granddaughter of Judge Thompson, her father being the late John K. Pickering of Portsmouth, N. H., son of Richard and Mary (Thompson) Pickering of Newington.

settlers of New Hampshire, and owner of all the south end of Portsmouth then known as "Pickering's Neck." He had also 500 acres of land on the beautiful shore of the Great Bay in Newington, a large part of which descended to Mrs. Thompson's grandfather, Thomas Pickering, who added thereto, and left a large farm to each of his six sons, among whom was John Gee Pickering, her father.

Benjamin Thompson was an extensive land-owner in Durham and Barrington. For twenty years in early life he was clerk of the Court of Common Pleas in Strafford county, and was also Justice of the Peace. He inherited the Thompson homestead estate, where he established his oldest son Ebenezer (father of the present writer), who was succeeded by a son of the same honored name, by whom it was bequeathed to his youngest son, Lucien Thompson, the present owner. Here at least seven generations of the family have lived.

V. *Mary*, or "Polly," as she is called in her father's will, b. April 11, 1767 ; d. Oct. 10, 1837. She married, Nov. 8, 1787, Richard Pickering, Esq., of Newington, an affluent and honorable member of the above mentioned family. It was with this, her favorite daughter, ended her days, Nov. 14, 1807, Mary Torr, widow of the Hon. Ebenezer Thompson.

JUDGE THOMPSON'S DESCENDANTS.

The descendants of Judge Thompson of the name may be divided into two branches. I. That of Col. Ebenezer Thompson of Portsmouth, N. H. II. That of Benjamin Thompson, Esq., of Durham.

I.

The Line of Col. Ebenezer Thompson of Portsmouth.

Ebenezer Thompson

COL. EBENEZER THOMPSON[3] (son of Judge Ebenezer,[2] of Robert[1]), b. July 12, 1762; d. Feb. 4, 1828; m., *first*, January, 1786, Martha Burleigh, daughter of John and Anne (Hilton) Burleigh of New Market, who was born Aug. 29, 1769; died in 1796.

Children:

I. JOHN BURLEIGH[4], b. Nov. 21, 1786; d. Oct. 7, 1810. Unmarried.

II. ANNE HILTON,[4] b. Sept. 19, 1789; d. 1812. Unmarried.

III. MARY,[4] b. in Durham, Feb. 24, 1792; d. in Portsmouth, N. H., March 28, 1865.

IV. MARTHA,[4] b. Dec. 12, 1795; d. May 8, 1706.

Of these four children, Mary alone was married. She became the second wife of the Hon. William Claggett, a prominent politician in early life,—a representative and senator, and the naval officer at Portsmouth from 1830 to 1838. His first wife was Sarah, daughter of Gov. William Plumer, who died Sept. 18, 1818. William Claggett was born in Litchfield, N. H., in 1790; died in Portsmouth, Dec. 28, 1870. He was the son of the Hon. Wyseman Claggett, who was born, August, 1721, at the manor of Broad Oaks, near Bristol, England. He was educated in that country, and admitted a barrister in the Court of the King's Bench. He afterwards came to America, and established himself at Portsmouth, N. H., where in 1767 he was appointed the king's Attorney-General for the province. Before the Revolution he removed to Litchfield, where he owned a large and valuable estate on the Merrimack. He strongly advocated the rights of the colonies, and at the Revolutionary period was a member of the Committee of Safety, and aided in carrying into effect the first temporary form of government for the state of New Hampshire, under which he held the office of Solicitor-General, and was one of the Executive Council. He was thus brought into constant connection with Judge Thompson, and they were personal friends. He died in Litchfield, Dec. 4, 1784.

William Claggett had several children by his second marriage, four of whom lived to maturity. Three of these died early and unmarried. The only survivor is William, who now resides in New York.

Col. Thompson married, *secondly*, May 4, 1797, Mary Weeks of Greenland, b. May 8, 1770; d. Nov. 15, 1813. They had six children:

V. EBENEZER,[4] b. in Durham, Feb. 5, 1798; d. at midnight, Jan. 26–27, 1853; m. his cousin, Ann Mary, daughter of Benjamin Thompson, Esq., who was born Aug. 8, 1809; d. one hour after her husband, Jan. 27, 1853. He was for many years master of a merchant vessel to foreign ports, and was generally called "Captain Eben Thompson." About 1834 he purchased the mansion formerly owned by Gen. John Sullivan, on the bank of the Oyster river, in Durham, where he resided till his death. He was a member of the New Hampshire legislature in 1845 and 1846, and one of the leading members of the Congregational church in Durham.

VI. MARTHA WEEKS,[4] b. in Durham, Nov. 25, 1799; d. in Barrington, N. H., Feb. 1, 1855; m., September, 1827, Benjamin Odiorne, who was born in Rochester, N. H., Jan. 16, 1801; d. in Barrington, Aug. 29, 1872. One child, *Mary*, unmarried.

VII. JACOB WEEKS,[4] b. in Durham, Jan. 2, 1802; d. at his residence in Portsmouth, July 7, 1864; m., Nov. 3, 1829, Artemisia Rindge of Portsmouth, who was born July 13, 1801; d. July 31, 1866. He was for many years master of a vessel in the merchant service, and was generally known as "Captain Jacob Thompson."

VIII. BENJAMIN,[4] b. in Portsmouth, March 31, 1804; d. in Barrington, N. H., April 23, 1875; m. Lucinda J. Drew of Barrington, Dec. 23, 1833. She was born Nov. 29, 1812; d. Feb. 22, 1862.

IX. GEORGE WEEKS,[4] b. in Portsmouth, March 29, 1807; m., April 18, 1833, Mary, daughter of Deacon John Wingate, of Stratham, in which town she was born. Nov. 2, 1810. Her grandfather was the Rev. and Hon. Paine Wingate, a distinguished statesman of New Hampshire,—Member of Congress, and Judge of the Superior Court, whose wife was Eunice Pickering, sister of the Hon. Timothy Pickering of Massachusetts, Quartermaster-General of the Continental army.

The Rev. George W. Thompson studied for the ministry at the Gilmanton Theological Seminary (N. H.), where he was graduated in 1839. He was ordained in Kingston, N. H., April 29, 1840. After thirteen years spent in the exercise of his profession at Dracut and Carlisle, Mass., he retired to his estate in Stratham, N. H., where, preaching occasionally, he continues to reside. No children.

X. HANNAH ELEANOR WEEKS,[4] twin sister of the Rev. Geo. W. Thompson, b. March 29, 1807; m., Aug. 13, 1827, Dr. Josiah Bartlett of Stratham (b. May 3, 1803; d. May 13, 1853), grandson of the Hon. Josiah Bartlett, one of the signers of the Declaration of Independence, and the first governor of New Hampshire.

Children of Capt. Ebenezer Thompson[4] (son of Col. Ebenezer,[3] of Judge Ebenezer,[2] of Robert[1]), all of whom were born in the Sullivan house, Durham, N. H. :

I. CHARLES AUGUSTUS COFFIN,[5] b. July 20, 1835 ; d. Dec. 4, 1868.

II. WILLIAM HALE,[5] b. May 9, 1838.

III. BENJAMIN,[5] b. June 7, 1845 ; d. July 27, 1845.

CHARLES AUGUSTUS COFFIN THOMP-
SON[5] (son of Capt. Ebenezer,[4] of Col. Ebenezer,[3] of
Judge Ebenezer,[2] of Robert[1]), was born in Durham,
N. H., July 20, 1835 ; died Dec. 4, 1868. He inherited, among other property, the paternal mansion, in
which he always resided. December 25, 1855, he
married Louisa J. Davis (born July 21, 1834), a descendant of John Davis, one of the early settlers at
Oyster River, whose children and grandchildren suffered so severely in the various attacks by the Indians. Her paternal grandmother was Judith Tuttle,
a descendant of John Tuttle of Dover, Judge of the
Superior Court in 1695, and for many years subse-
quent.

Children :

I. GEORGE EBENEZER,[6] b. Dec. 15, 1859; graduated at the
Chandler Scientific School, Hanover, N. H., June, 1879,
and at the Harvard Medical College in 1882. Now a practitioner of medicine in Boston, Mass.

II. ADA MARY,[6] b. Nov. 11, 1862 ; graduated at Wellesley
College, Mass., June, 1886.

III. HELEN FRANCES,[6] b. Sept. 21, 1867.

COL. WILLIAM HALE THOMPSON,[5] (son of Capt. Ebenezer,[4] of Col. Ebenezer,[3] of Judge Ebenezer,[2] of Robert[1]), was born in Durham, N. H., May 9, 1838. He attended school at the Merrimack Institute, Reed's Ferry, N. H., and afterwards at Phillips Exeter Academy. At the death of his parents in .1853 he went to Portsmouth to reside with his uncle, Capt. Jacob W. Thompson, who was his guardian. In 1854 he went to sea in the "Emily Farnum," as a mere sailor before the mast, although he had inherited a handsome property; and went around Cape Horn three times. At the age of seventeen he was appointed second officer, and discharged his duties in so efficient a manner that he would, at the proper age, have been at the head of his profession. But in 1856, while in port at San Francisco, Cal., he fell into the hold of his vessel, and crushed his left arm to such a degree that amputation was thought necessary. He stoutly resisted this measure, preferring death, as he said, to the loss of his arm. By this means it was saved; but for a long time he was unable to use it, and was, of course, obliged to quit the service. He then entered the counting-room of Cummings & Lee, East India commission merchants, one of the largest mercantile houses in Boston, Mass. Here he remained till the beginning of the late civil war, to the entire satisfaction of the firm. It was during this time that he acquired a taste for military affairs; and in 1857 he joined the well known company of "Boston Tigers," then under the command of Capt. Charles O. Rogers, serving as a private with such men as Gen. Thomas Stevenson, "the best volunteer soldier in the army of the Potomac," as Gen. Burnside called him, and Gen. Miles, afterwards prominent in the conflicts with the Indians.

At the breaking out of the civil war he was offered the choice of three positions,—that of quartermaster in the regular army, of a captaincy in the Ninth Infantry, also in the regular service, or that of paymaster in the U. S. Navy. The Hon. John P. Hale, then chairman of the U. S. Senate Naval Committee, persuaded him to take the appointment in the navy. He was examined by the U. S. Naval Board, New York, Aug. 21, 1861, and out of thirty-six appointments had the second place. August 23 he received his commission as assistant paymaster, U. S. N., with the rank of lieutenant, and was ordered, Oct. 2, 1861, to the sloop of war "Mohican," belonging to Admiral Dupont's squadron, which sailed from New York Oct. 20, 1861, and took part in the battle of Port Royal, S. C., Nov. 7, 1861, the capture of Fernandina, Fla., and the taking of other seaports along the South Atlantic coast, and was in many engagements at Fort Sumpter. July 2, 1862, he was promoted to the office of full Paymaster, with the rank of Lieut. Commander, and ordered to report to Admiral David G. Farragut, for duty on board the U. S. frigate "Susquehanna," the flag-ship of the Western Division, commanded by Commodore Hitchcock. He remained in this squadron till May, 1863, participating in all of Admiral Farragut's naval engagements during that period. June 30, 1863, he was ordered to report to Admiral S. P. Lee, then in command of the North Atlantic squadron, on board the U. S. frigate " Brandywine," for such duty as might be assigned to him. He was ordered to undertake the duties of Fleet Paymaster, to relieve Commander C. J. Emery, who turned over to him sixteen small ships of war in the James river, which number, after Admiral Porter took command of the squadron, was increased to fifty vessels during that cruise, many of them separated months at a time, and at least a hundred miles distant. His returns to the U. S. Treasury Department show that his responsibilities at that time were greater than those of any other disbursing officer in the U. S. Navy ; and his accounts were settled so entirely to the satisfaction of the U. S. Treasurer that he received a letter from the Fourth Auditor of the Treasury, saying that he deserved special credit for the discharge of his multiplied duties under such unusually difficult circumstances.

March 10, 1866, Paymaster Thompson received orders to report for duty as Naval Storekeeper at St. Paul de Loanda, on the coast of Africa, where our government vessels get supplies ; but through the influence of his family he was induced to resign his office March 30, 1866, and leave the navy. In April, 1868, he went to Chicago, and engaged in the real estate business. He bought several tracts of land, and erected a number of large buildings, among others "Thompson's Block," on West Madison street, with a frontage of 252 feet, which was the best building left in Chicago after the great fire.

Col. Thompson was twice chosen by the Republican party to represent his district in the Illinois legislature (1877 and 1878), and served in the 30th and 31st General Assemblies, where he accomplished much for his constituents. He procured the passage of several important bills, such as the " Back-tax Bill," which enabled the city of Chicago to secure $3,000,000 from delinquents, and the " Bill for Prevention of Cruelty to Animals." It was through his exertions that the first " Military-Law Bill " in Illinois was passed, and the consequent establishment of the Illinois National Guards who did so much in 1877 to quell the riots in Chicago, which threatened the destruction of the city. He was one of the wealthiest members in the house ; and being a man of fine presence, cordial manners, and ready wit, could not fail to be popular. And like his grandfather, Col. Thompson of Portsmouth, N. H., whom he resembles so strongly in character, he has a fluency of speech that speedily gained him a reputation for eloquence. A Chicago journal of that time says,—"As an orator he stands first on the Republican side. His celebrated speech on the militia bill was a piece of splendid composition and magnificently delivered, and it established his reputation." In recognition of his services for the military, Gov. Cullom appointed him one of his aides-de-camp, July 2, 1877, with the rank of colonel. May 10, 1879, he was chosen lieutenant-colonel, in command of the Sixth Battalion of the Illinois National Guards. In April, 1881, he was chosen colonel of the Sixth Regiment of the Illinois National Guards. He resigned his office in the Guards May 24, 1884, on account of the pressure of private business.

Col. Thompson married, in Exeter, N. H., Jan. 26, 1864, Medora Gale (b. in Chicago, March 16, 1843), daughter of Mr. Stephen F. Gale of Chicago and of his wife, Medora A., the daughter of the Hon. Theophilus Smith, for many years Judge of the Supreme Court of Illinois.

Children :

I. HELEN GALE,[6] born in Portsmouth, N. H., Jan. 12, 1866.

II. WILLIAM HALE,[6] born in Boston, Mass., May 14, 1867.

III. GALE,[6] born in Chicago, Ill., Jan. 12, 1871.

IV. PERCIVAL,[6] born in Chicago, Sept. 26, 1876.

Children of Capt. Jacob W. Thompson[4] (son of Col. Ebenezer,[3] of Judge Ebenezer,[2] of Robert[1]), all of whom were born in Portsmouth, N. H. :

I. ANNIE WEEKS,[5] b. March 1, 1832; m. Dr. Frank Fuller, of New York city, Dec. 14, 1870.

II. JACOB HALE,[5] b. April 9, 1837; graduated at Bowdoin college, Brunswick, Me., in the class of 1860. Now one of the editors of the *New York Times*.

III. MARY ELISABETH,[5] b. Dec. 26, 1838; m., Feb. 7, 1861, Capt. George B. Wendell, of Portsmouth, N. H., who was born Jan. 31, 1831; died Sept. 25, 1881, at Quincy, Mass., where his family still reside. Capt. Wendell, for many years, was master of a vessel in the East India trade. Six children.

IV. ISAAC RINDGE,[5] b. March 25, 1842; resides in Quincy, Mass.

Children of Benjamin Thompson[4] (son of Col. Ebenezer,[3] of Judge Ebenezer,[2] of Robert[1]):

I. GEORGE WEEKS,[5] b. March 31, 1837. A volunteer in the late civil war, serving as a private in Co. F, Seventh Regt. of Infantry. Mortally wounded at Morris Island, S. C., July 28, 1863, and died the following day, aged 26. Unmarried.

II. JOSIAH BARTLETT,[5] b. Nov. 8, 1839. Served in the navy, under Admiral Farragut, in the civil war ; was at the battle of Vicksburg, etc. Married Ida F. Fuller, Aug. 6, 1873. Died in Madison, Dakota, March 16, 1882. No children.

III. JONATHAN DREW,[5] b. Nov. 27, 1841. He was a volunteer in the civil war, in Co. F., Thirteenth Regt. Died at the hospital, Washington, D. C., Dec. 30, 1862, aged 21. Unmarried.

IV. MARY ELIZABETH WEEKS,[5] b. Sept. 6, 1843 ; m. Albion P. Nichols, of Searsport, Me., Jan. 22, 1873 ; resides in Hamlet, Ill. Two children.

V. ANNIE WEEKS,[5] b. Sept. 7, 1847 ; m. William P. Ray, Dec. 8, 1868 ; resides in Faneuil, Mass. Two children.

VI. MARTHA AURELIA,[5] b. Nov. 16, 1854 ; m. Jacob S. Nichols, brother of the above Albion P., June 13, 1877 ; resides in Marseilles, Ill. Two children.

II.

The Line of Benjamin Thompson, Esq., of Durham, N. H.

BENJAMIN THOMPSON[3] (son of Judge Eben-
ezer,[2] of Robert[1]), b. March 31, 1765; d. Jan. 21,
1838; m., May 11, 1794, Mary Pickering of Newington, who was born June 15, 1774; died Oct. 1, 1849.
Children (all born in Durham):

I. EBENEZER,[4] b. Nov. 22, 1795; d. Oct. 12, 1796.

II. EBENEZER,[4] b. July 25, 1797; d. April 22, 1826; m. Jane
Demerit, Aug. 16, 1820.

III. JOHN,[4] b. Feb. 5, 1799; d. Aug. 24, 1800.

IV. JOHN,[4] b. Dec. 2, 1801; entered Phillips Exeter Academy
in 1815; graduated at Harvard University in 1822. Studied law with the Hon. Levi Woodbury, Portsmouth, N. H.,
and established himself as a lawyer at Centre Harbor, N. H.,
as early as October, 1825. Died Jan. 22, 1854. Unmarried. He inherited from his father, among other property,
the " Beech Hill farm," in Durham.

V. BENJAMIN,[4] b. April 22, 1806. He inherited, among other
property, his father's residence in Durham village, with
neighboring lands, and the so-called "Warner farm," originally a part of the Valentine Hill grant at Oyster River.

VI. ANN MARY, b. Aug. 8, 1809; d. Jan. 27, 1853; m. Capt.
Ebenezer Thompson, Dec. 15, 1831. Part of her inherit-
ance was the "Long Marsh farm," a tract of land called
by that name as early as February, 17$\frac{2}{3}\frac{0}{1}$, as appears from
the town records of Durham. This farm descended to her
son, Col. Wm. H. Thompson of Chicago.

(For her children, see Line of Col. Thompson of Portsmouth, page 61, etc.)

Of the foregoing children of Benjamin and Mary (Pickering) Thompson, the only son with issue was

EBENEZER THOMPSON,[4] b. July 25, 1797 ; d. April 22, 1826, aged 28. He entered Phillips Exeter Academy in 1809, and showed great aptitude for study, especially mathematics, in which he was a proficient at an unusually early age. He had a good business capacity, and was a genial, popular man. He was a Justice of the Peace, and at the age of twenty-six was chosen, March 9, 1824, chairman of the board of selectmen of Durham, which office he held till his death. He married, Aug. 16, 1820, Jane, daughter of Nathaniel Demerit and of Mary McCrillis his wife, who was born Nov. 12, 1794, and died, after forty-one years of widowhood, at her residence in Durham village, May 26, 1869. He settled on the Thompson homestead at his marriage, and he and his wife lie buried beside Judge Thompson, in the private burying-ground where at least six generations of the family have been interred.

Ancestry of Jane, wife of Ebenezer Thompson, Esq.

JANE DEMERIT, wife of Ebenezer Thompson, descended from Elie or Ely de Merit, a Huguenot refugee, who came to this country from the Isle of Jersey shortly after the revocation of the Edict of Nantes, and had a grant of land in the township of Dover, N. H., April 11, 1694. He married, as early as 1695, Hopestill or Hope ———, and died about 1747, in which year his son Eli ceased to add "Junior" to his name. He seems, by his will, to have left an estate in the Isle of Jersey, where the family had first taken refuge.*

Of the five children of Ely,[1] the oldest was Eli,[2] b. March 1, 1696; d. May 5, 1774; m., as early as 1722, Tabitha, daughter of Derry Pitman of Oyster River, who was baptized, together with her infant son Samuel, by the Rev. Hugh Adams, April 12, 1724. Eli[2] was one of the selectmen of Dover for thirteen years, if no more, between 1736 and 1753, and of Madbury for three years, after the incorporation of that town in 1755. It was to him that the town-

---

*It is uncertain how the name of Demerit was originally written. It was probably modified in this country, like most foreign names, to suit English ears. Mr. Baird gives De Marest, De Marée, and Méric, which are not dissimilar in pronunciation. The Rev. Hugh Adams of Oyster River, to whose parish Eli[1] seems to have belonged, writes it "De Merit" in his Church Records in 1724. I find it so written in a deed of land in Rochester, in 1756, from "John De Merit Jr." of Madbury. And I have in my possession a deed of June 12, 1760, in which "Samuel De Merett" pays £170, old tenor, for a pew in Madbury meeting-house. By the family, it has been variously written—Demerit, Demeritt, and De Meritt.

ship of Peeling, N. H., was originally granted, Sept. 23, 1763.

Capt. Samuel Demerit,[3] the oldest son of Eli,[2] was born May 8, 1723; died Oct. 22, 1770. He married, *first*, Elizabeth Randall (baptized "an infant" by the Rev. Hugh Adams, April 21, 1728; died June 20, 1767), daughter of Capt. Nathaniel Randall of that part of Durham now called Lee, where he erected mills and built the "Randall garrison," which served as a refuge to the neighborhood in times of danger from the Indians.* Her portion of her father's estate consisted of one hundred acres of land in Nottingham (No. 25, Winter street), and one whole right in Canterbury, together with a house lot in that town.

Samuel Demerit settled on his father's lands in Durham, still owned by his descendants. Sept. 29, 1755, he received from Gov. Benning Wentworth the commission of Quartermaster in Col. John Downing's regiment of troopers, and was very efficient in raising and equipping men for the Seven Years' War, as testified by old documents now in the writer's possession. April 5, 1765, he received from Gov. Wentworth the commission of Captain in the Seventh Troop of Horse, Col. Clement March's regiment, and

*A slave of Capt. Nathaniel Randall's served in Col. Hercules Mooney's regiment in 1758. His name is entered in the roll as "Cesar Durham, negro."

raised a company of " Gentlemen Troopers " in Durham and vicinity. His son Samuel served as a private in Capt. Winborn Adams's company, that went
from Durham in 1775 to join the continental army.

Of the ten children of Capt. Samuel Demerit by
his first marriage, the oldest son who lived to grow
up was Nathaniel, b. Oct. 26, 1751 ; d. Jan. 18, 1827.
He received from Gen. John Sullivan, then President
of New Hampshire, the commission of First Lieutenant in the Second Regiment of the New Hampshire
militia. He married, June 19, 1783, Mary McCrillis
of Nottingham, N. H., where she was born April 9,
1756; died in Durham, Sept. 3, 1847. She was of
pure Scotch descent, being the daughter of William
McCrillis and of Jean Kelsey his wife, who were both
born in the north of Ireland of Scotch parents, with
whom they came to this country in their childhood.
Of the six children of Nathaniel and Mary Demerit,*
the fifth was Jane, wife of Ebenezer Thompson.

On the maternal side, Mrs. Thompson's grand-
parents were John McCrillis and Margaret Burnside,
who were married in Londonderry, Ireland, not far
from the year 1700. In that place all their children
were born. They were both Scotch, or of Scotch
parentage. At the death of his wife, John McCrillis

---

* Their only son, the Rev. William Demeritt, was founder of
the " Christian church " in Durham, as well as of the Durham
academy, so prosperous during his lifetime.

came to America with six of his children, if no more,
leaving behind one married daughter, Mrs. Jean
Henrie or Henry. They sailed from Port Rush,
Aug. 7, 1726, together with other Scotch-Irish emigrants, such as the McClarys, Harveys, Kelseys, and
Simpsons (all of whom settled in Nottingham), and
arrived at Boston October 8 following. John Mc-
Crillis bought two "home lotts" in Nottingham of
George St. Clare for £100, on which he settled as
early as 1734. Unlike most of the Scotch-Irish emigrants, he was a member of the Church of England;
and the rector of the Episcopal church in Portsmouth
went to Nottingham more than once to baptize his
grandchildren. His son, John McCrillis,[2] who settled in Deerfield, N. H., married Margaret Harvey.[*]
A daughter of theirs became the wife of Major Andrew McClary, who was afterwards killed at Bunker
Hill.

William McCrillis,[2] son of John McCrillis,[1] married
Jean Kelsey. One of their children was Mary, wife
of Lieut. Nathaniel Demerit, and another was William, who was mortally wounded at the battle of Bunker Hill.

---

[*]Among the descendants of John McCrillis[2] is the Hon.
Wm. H. McCrillis of Bangor, the wealthiest lawyer in Maine.
He was delegate to the Republican convention at Chicago
that nominated Lincoln and Hamlin as President and Vice-
President of the United States, and was chosen one of the com-
mittee to notify Mr. Lincoln of his nomination.

Of the daughters of John McCrillis,[1] Martha, married Capt. Hugh Morrison, who settled in Coleraine, Mass., where he built a fortified house, noted in the early history of that town as " Hugh Morrison's fort." David, the oldest son of Hugh Morrison and Martha McCrillis, was taken captive by the Indians July 28, 1746, and his fate was never known. Their daughter Martha, the first white child born in Coleraine (June 29, 1740), married Hugh, son of Dr. Hugh Bolton of England, and of Elizabeth Patterson his wife, of the family that afterwards went to Baltimore and became noted for the marriage of one of its members with Jerome Bonaparte.[*]

Another daughter of John McCrillis,[1] named Mary, married John Henrie or Henry, one of the most prominent and influential of the early settlers of Coleraine. She had previously been married to Mr. Workman of Colerain, Ireland, where he died, leaving one son, also named John, who came to this country with his mother and settled in Coleraine, Mass. John Workman did good service in the Seven Years' War, in 1755 and 1756. Among his descendants may be mentioned Dr. William Workman, a surgeon in the late civil war, who died in 1885, in

---

[*]I make this statement on the authority of the late Mr. Hugh Bolton Miller of Coleraine, a lineal descendant of Dr. Bolton and Elizabeth Patterson, who was profoundly versed in the history of that town and the pedigree of its inhabitants.

Worcester, Mass., in his eighty-eighth year. Another is Mrs. Alger, wife of the present governor of Michigan.*

Mrs. Jane Thompson was named for her maternal grandmother Jean (Kelsey) McCrillis, daughter of William Kelsey and of Margaret Hay his wife, both natives of Ireland, but of Scotch parentage. One of their sons, Hugh Kelsey, was killed at the siege of Louisbourg in 1745. Another son, Moses, served in the Seven Years' War; first, as a sergeant in Capt. Shepherd's company, Col. Nathaniel Meserve's regiment, which was sent from New Hampshire in 1756 to operate against the French around Lake Champlain. In 1757 he belonged, apparently as quartermaster, to one of the companies detached from Col. Meserve's regiment to join the Earl of Loudon's expedition against Louisbourg.** He afterwards served in New York, where he was slain some time in the year 1758.

One of Mrs. McCrillis's sisters, Sarah Kelsey, mar-

---

* The writer has in her possession two letters from Mrs. Jean Henric, written from Ireland in 1752 to her father, John McCrillis of Nottingham, and her brother of the same name, in which she asks if they have had "any account of brother Hugh Morrison's sone that was taken away by the Engens," and "what is become of little John Workman."

** During this campaign, Sergeant or Quartermaster Kelsey kept a brief diary with valuable memoranda, including the roll of his company, which is in the possession of his great-grandniece, the present writer.

ried Thomas Allison, an early settler of Barrington, where he discovered iron ore on his land, and erected a forge for the manufacture of iron utensils for the use of the colonists till a better quality could be obtained. They were the great-grandparents of Gen. Benjamin F. Butler, ex-governor of Massachusetts.

Another sister, Mary, married James Morrison of Nottingham. One of their sons, also named James, was a captain in the Revolutionary army, and a member of Gen. Lee's body-guard. Another son, Robert, rendered good service at Bunker Hill, Saratoga, and Stillwater. He was with Major Andrew McClary when the latter was slain at Bunker Hill, and received that gallant officer in his arms when he fell. A son of his, the Hon. Robert Morrison of Portsmouth, N. H. (born June 30, 1797), died in Northwood, N. H., Nov. 23, 1884.

Children of Ebenezer Thompson[4] and of Jane Demerit his wife :

I. EBENEZER,[5] b. Aug. 15, 1821 ; d. May 15, 1869 ; m., Sept. 26, 1843, Nancy G. Carr of New London, N. H. He inherited the Thompson homestead, where he established himself at his marriage, and where all his children were born.

II. WILLIAM,[5] b. Oct. 27, 1823 ; d. May 7, 1859 ; m., Jan. 1, 1845, Mary Jane Chapman of New Market, who was born Oct. 24, 1824 ; died May 20, 1852. He inherited the so-called " Torr farm," on Mast road, in Durham. Like his father, he was a man of fine physical proportions, and of a genial, generous nature, with much humor and originality of expression. He left no children.

III. MARY PICKERING,[5] born Nov. 19, 1825. The compiler of this Record.

Of the children of Ebenezer Thompson[4] and Jane Demerit, the only one who left issue was

EBENEZER THOMPSON,[5] b. Aug. 15, 1821 ; d. May 15, 1869. He was a man of keen, active mind and intellectual tastes. He was specially familiar with the early history of the New England colonies, and began to collect materials for the history of Durham. He was shrewd and energetic in business, frugal and laborious in his habits, and carefully solicitous for the welfare of his family. He took a strong interest in politics, and held several town offices. In 1855 he was first selectman and town treasurer, and for several years was overseer of the poor. He was appointed Justice of the Peace for the county of Strafford by Gov. Metcalf, July 13, 1855. He was greatly interested in the public schools, and was so efficient a superintendent that he received a vote of thanks at the annual town-meeting in 1861 " for his assiduity, and interest taken, and zeal manifested, in the cause of common schools in this town,"—one of the few votes of a similar nature in the whole town records.

Ebenezer Thompson married, Sept. 26, 1843, Nancy Greeley Carr of New London, N. H., daughter of Capt. Samuel Carr (or Ker, as the name was originally written) and of Nancy Greeley his wife. On the paternal side, Mrs. Thompson descended from John and Elizabeth (Wilson) Ker, Scotch-Irish emigrants, who came to Chester, N. H., in 1736, bringing with them a valuable testimonial of their moral worth from their pastor in Ireland, of which the following is an exact copy from the original :—

" That John Ker and his wife Elisabeth Wilson lived within the bounds of this Congregation from their Infancy, behaveing themselves soberly, honestly and piously, free of any Publick Scandall, so that they may be received as members of any Cristian Congregation or Society where God in Providence may order their lott, is Certified at Ballywollen, June 23, 1736, by
" JA : THOMSON."

Mrs. Thompson's mother was the daughter of Jonathan Greeley, Esq., who settled in New London, N. H., in 1795. He was a man of great integrity, a leading member of the Baptist church, and one of the early benefactors to the academy of that town. Among his grandnephews is Lieut. A. W. Greely, the celebrated Arctic explorer. And the Hon. Horace Greeley, of the *New York Tribune*, descended from his uncle.

Children of Ebenezer and Nancy G. Thompson :

I. CLARENCE GREELEY,[6] b. April 13, 1845 ; d. in Manchester, N. H., Aug. 30, 1877.

II. ARTHUR[6], b. Sept. 20, 1846; d. Nov. 10, 1846.

III. ELLA PICKERING[6], b. Dec. 11, 1847 ; d. at the Thompson homestead, June 15, 1882. She married, May 15, 1881, the Hon. Joshua B. Smith, of Durham, for many years prominent in the affairs of the town, holding the chief offices, and representing it in the legislature for four years. He was also a member of the state senate, and belonged to the governor's council. He descended from Joseph Smith, who built the Smith garrison at Oyster River that escaped destruction in the Indian attack of 1694.

The following notice of Mrs. Smith appeared in the Dover *Enquirer* of June 29, 1882 :

"In Durham, June 15, Mrs. Ella P. Smith, wife of Hon. Joshua B. Smith, and daughter of the late Ebenezer Thompson, Esq., aged thirty-four years and six months. This lady was widely and favorably known as an amateur artist of great merit, and her death cannot fail to excite much regret among her numerous friends and acquaintances. She received her art education at the celebrated School of Design, Cooper Union, New York, where she was sent as soon as she had completed a thorough course of English studies. Here she at once attracted the notice of Dr. Rimmer, the director of the school, who took special pains in developing her talent and giving her the knowledge of art-anatomy for which her productions are distinguished. In 1869 she received the highest prize of the school, sixty dollars in gold, for "St. Stephen," an original painting in oil. The following year she painted "The Beggar Maid," remarkable for its rich Rembrandt-like coloring; and executed from the live model her much admired statuette, "The Water Baby," suggested by Charles Kingsley's fairy tale of "The Water Babies." The graceful pose and anatomical correctness of this statuette attracted the attention of Frank Leslie, the well known journalist, who purchased the first copy.

"Miss Thompson subsequently resided several years in Manchester, N. H., where she excited interest on account of her exceptional artistic talent, and her many admirable traits of character. She became a prominent member of the Manchester Art Association, and several of her works were exhibited in Music Hall, at the state fair of 1874, having the post of honor, and obtained for her a silver medal from the Agricultural Society. Soon after, she had a studio on Tremont street, Boston, where, among other works, she executed a fine bas-relief of the "Madonna and Child," and a statuette, "Mother and child." Several of her productions are to be seen in the art rooms at Manchester. They have a character much above the common grade of amateur art, and give proofs of genuine originality. In fact, she seldom copied the works of others, but produced original designs indicative of a lively imagination well directed by the rules of art, and a decided creative talent that bade fair to render her distinguished.

" Returning to her native place, Miss Thompson was married to Mr. Smith, May 15, 1881. In domestic life she showed the excellent judgment and practical good sense that always distinguished her. She was not only capable of directing others, but was well skilled herself in every branch of housewifery, the knowledge of which she regarded as the true woman's highest accomplishment ; and she seemed to ennoble the lowest household duties by the very manner in which she performed them.

" She joined the Congregational church at Durham in 1869, and, though unostentatious in her piety, had strong religious convictions ; and her moral influence was constantly felt by those brought in contact with her.

" In social life Mrs. Smith was most valued where she was best known. Her mental qualities were of a high order, her tastes were refined and elevated, her friendships generous and strong, and her sudden death in the prime of life leaves a sad void in the circle of her relatives and friends."

Mrs. Smith left one child,—

Ella Thompson[7], b. June 15, 1882 ; d. Oct. 23, 1882.

IV. FRANCIS,[6] b. Feb. 23, 1849 ; d. Sept. 16, 1849.

V. ANNIE LOUISE,[6] b. June 8, 1857.

VI. LUCIEN,[6] b. June 3, 1859. He inherited the Thompson homestead, where he resides, and, with the exception of his great uncle, who is unmarried, is now the only male representative of Benjamin Thompson's line.

www.ingramcontent.com/pod-product-compliance
Lightning Source LLC
Chambersburg PA
CBHW020048030726
47499CB00007B/2633